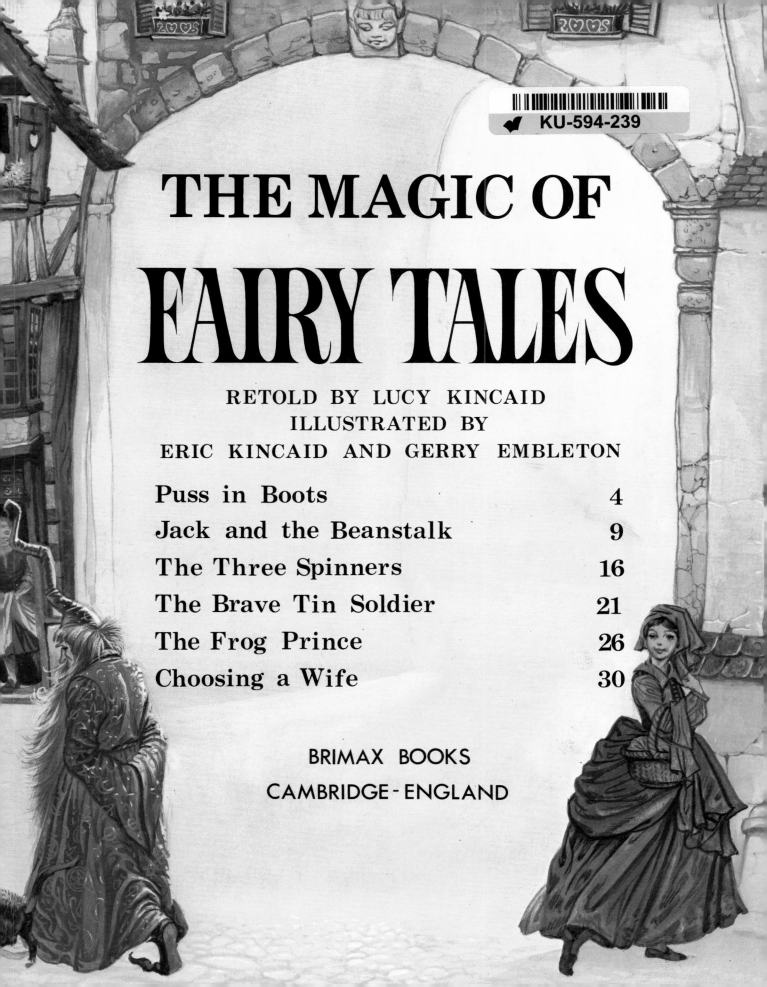

THE MAGIC OF
FAIRY TALES

RETOLD BY LUCY KINCAID
ILLUSTRATED BY
ERIC KINCAID AND GERRY EMBLETON

BRIMAX BOOKS

CAMBRIDGE - ENGLAND

Puss in Boots

Once upon a time, there was a miller, who had three sons. When he died he left his mill to his first son, his donkey to his second son, and because he had nothing else, he left his cat to his third son.

The first son ground flour at the mill and sold it. The second son harnessed the donkey to a cart and carried things for paying customers. But what could the third son do with a cat, except let him sit in the sun, and purr, and drink milk?

One day, the cat said, "Master, give me a pair of boots and a sack and you will see that I am not as useless as you think." It was a very strange request for a cat to make, but it was granted nonetheless.

The cat, or Puss in Boots, as the miller's son now called him, went into the forest and caught a rabbit. He put it in the sack and then instead of taking it home to the miller's son, he took it to the King's palace.

"Please accept this small present from my master the Marquis of Carabas," said Puss in Boots.

It was to be the first of many presents Puss in Boots took to the King, and each time he said he had been sent by his master the Marquis of Carabas. And though the King never actually met the Marquis of Carabas, he soon became very familiar with his name. The miller's son knew nothing of the presents, or of the Marquis of Carabas, and Puss in Boots didn't tell him.

One day, when Puss in Boots was at the palace, he overheard someone say that the King was about to take his daughter for a drive in the country. Puss in Boots hurried home.

"Quick master!" he called. "Go and bathe in the river and I will make your fortune."

It was another strange request for a cat to make but the miller's son was used to his pet by now and so he did as he was told. No sooner was he in the river than Puss in Boots took his clothes and threw them into the river with him.

"Puss . . . Puss . . . what are you doing?" called the miller's son.

Puss didn't answer, he was watching the road. Presently he saw the King's carriage in the distance. He waited until it was close then he ran out in the road in front of it.

"Help! Help! My master the Marquis of Carabas is drowning! Please save him!"

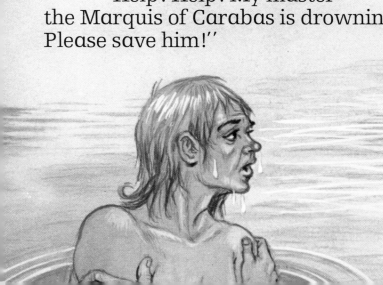

It took but a moment to drag the miller's son, who hadn't the slightest idea what Puss in Boots was up to, from the river and find him some dry clothes. He looked so handsome in the fine velvet tunic and the doublet and hose borrowed from one of the footmen that the princess fell in love with him at once.

"Father dear, may the Marquis of Carabas ride with us?"

The King liked to please his daughter and agreed to her request at once.

"Will you ride with us Puss?" asked the King.

Puss asked to be excused. He said he had something rather important to attend to. He ran on ahead of the carriage, and each time he saw someone at work in the fields he called,

"If the King asks who this land belongs to, tell him it belongs to the Marquis of Carabas."

The King did stop the carriage several times, and each time he received the same answer to his question.

'The Marquis of Carabas must be a very rich man,' he thought.

Puss in Boots ran so swiftly that soon he was a long way ahead of the carriage. Presently he came to a rich and imposing looking castle, which he knew belonged to a cruel and wicked ogre. He went straight up to the ogre without so much as a twitching of a whisker, and said,

"I hear you can turn yourself into any animal you choose. I won't believe a story like that unless I see it for myself."

Immediately, the ogre changed himself into a lion, and roared and growled and snarled.

"There . . ." he said, when he had turned himself back into an ogre. "I hope I frightened you."

"Must be easy to change yourself into something big," said Puss in Boots with a shrug. "I don't suppose you can turn yourself into something as small as a . . . er . . . um . . ." He seemed to be thinking. " . . . er . . . um . . . a mouse?"

The ogre couldn't have a mere cat doubting his special abilities. He changed himself into a tiny mouse in the twinkling of an eye. It was the last time he changed himself into anything because Puss in Boots pounced on him and ate him up before he could change back into an ogre, and THAT was the end of him!

"Hoorah!" shouted the castle servants. "We are free of the wicked ogre at last. Hoorah!"

"Your new master will always be kind, you can be sure of that," said Puss in Boots.

"Who IS our new master?" they asked.

"The Marquis of Carabas of course," said Puss.

When the King's carriage reached the castle, Puss in Boots was standing at the drawbridge, with the smiling servants gathered round him.

"Welcome . ." he said with a beautiful bow. "Welcome to the home of my master the Marquis of Carabas." The miller's son was too astonished to do anything except think to himself,

'Whatever is Puss up to?'

Luckily Puss had time to explain while the King was getting out of the carriage.

'What a rich man this Marquis must be,' thought the King. 'And such a nice young man too.'

Not long afterwards the princess and the miller's son were married. They, and Puss in Boots, lived happily ever after in the castle that had once belonged to the wicked ogre.

Jack and the Beanstalk

Jack lived with his mother in a tumble down house. They were so poor they never seemed to have enough to eat, and one day, Jack's mother said,

"Jack, you must take the cow to market and sell her."

"If I do that we will have no milk," said Jack.

"If we don't sell her we will soon have nothing to eat at all," replied his mother.

And so, very sadly, Jack led the cow to market. He was about half way there when he met an old man.

"Is your cow for sale?" asked the old man. Jack said that she was.

"Then I'll give you five beans for her," said the old man.

Jack laughed.

"You can't buy a cow with five beans," he said.

"Ah," said the old man, "But these are magic beans. You will make a fortune with them."

Jack couldn't resist such a good bargain. He gave the cow an affectionate pat, handed her halter to the old man, and took the five beans in exchange.

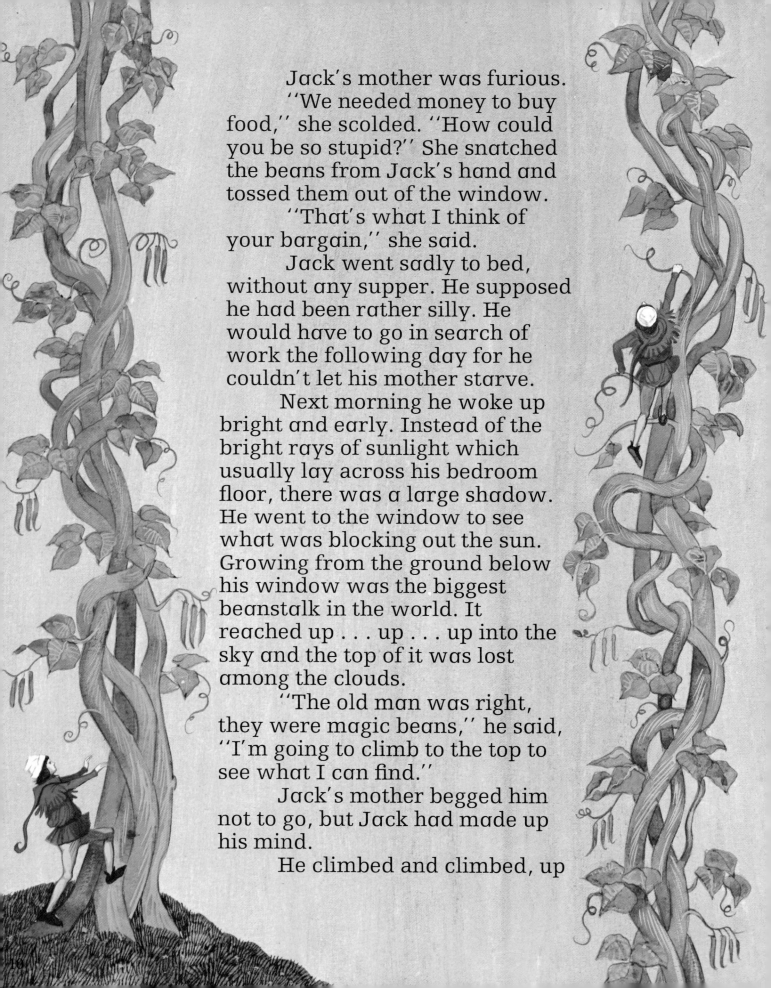

Jack's mother was furious. "We needed money to buy food," she scolded. "How could you be so stupid?" She snatched the beans from Jack's hand and tossed them out of the window.

"That's what I think of your bargain," she said.

Jack went sadly to bed, without any supper. He supposed he had been rather silly. He would have to go in search of work the following day for he couldn't let his mother starve.

Next morning he woke up bright and early. Instead of the bright rays of sunlight which usually lay across his bedroom floor, there was a large shadow. He went to the window to see what was blocking out the sun. Growing from the ground below his window was the biggest beanstalk in the world. It reached up . . . up . . . up into the sky and the top of it was lost among the clouds.

"The old man was right, they were magic beans," he said, "I'm going to climb to the top to see what I can find."

Jack's mother begged him not to go, but Jack had made up his mind.

He climbed and climbed, up

and up. He climbed through white swirling clouds until he came to the very tip of the beanstalk, and from the top of the beanstalk he stepped into another land. It was a land just like his own except that everything in it was twice and three times as big. All the climbing had made him hungry, so he went to the door of the only house he could see and knocked boldly. The door was opened by a huge woman. She was so big she was surely the wife of a giant. Jack persuaded her to give him some breakfast. He had just finished eating when he heard footsteps as heavy as falling boulders and then a voice as loud as thunder.

''FEE FI FO FUM, I SMELL THE BLOOD OF AN ENGLISHMAN!''

Quick as a flash, the giant woman bundled Jack into the oven.

''Sh . . . be very quiet,'' she said, ''That's my husband. He eats boys like you for breakfast.''

The huge woman, who was indeed the wife of a giant, told her husband he was mistaken and put a bowl of porridge on the table.

When he had eaten, the giant called for his hen.

"Lay!" he ordered. And the hen lay a golden egg.

Jack, who could see everything that was happening through a crack in the oven door, determined to have that hen for himself.

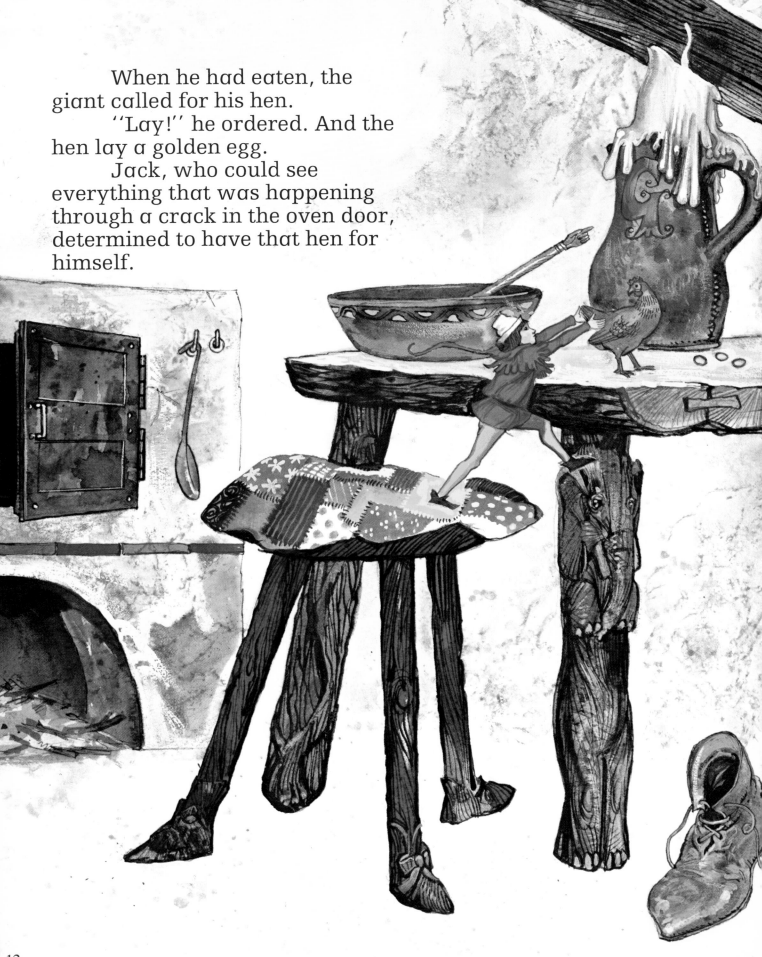

Presently the giant's head began to nod. Soon he was asleep. As quick as a bee about to sting, Jack left the oven, picked up the hen, ran to the top of the beanstalk and climbed down to earth again.

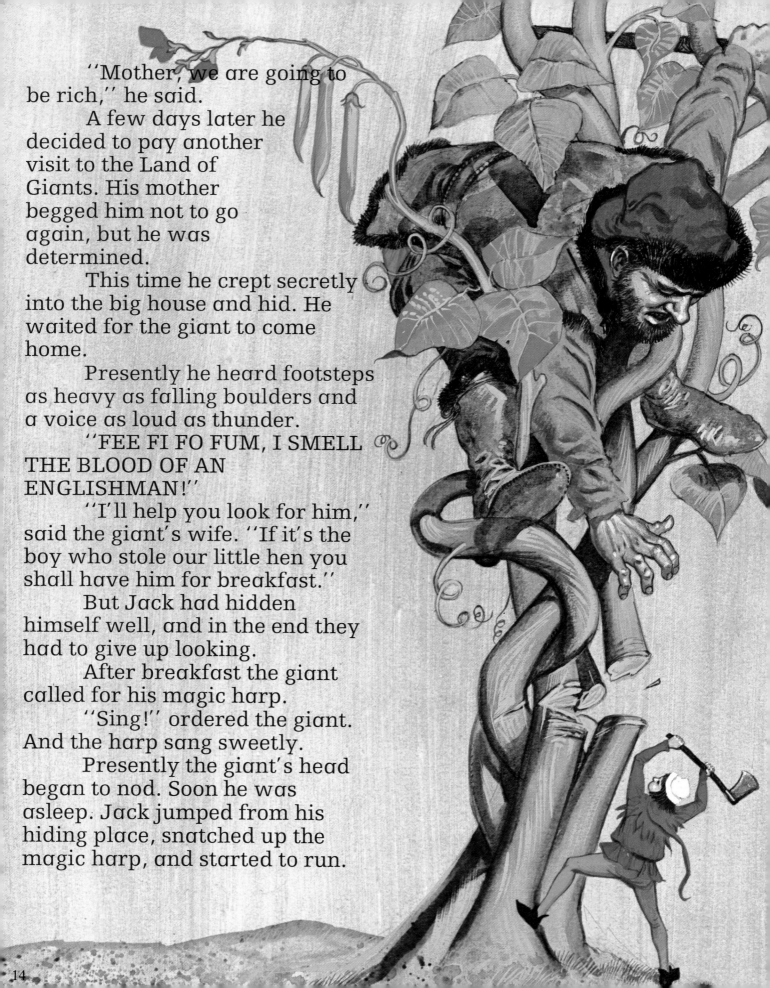

"Mother, we are going to be rich," he said.

A few days later he decided to pay another visit to the Land of Giants. His mother begged him not to go again, but he was determined.

This time he crept secretly into the big house and hid. He waited for the giant to come home.

Presently he heard footsteps as heavy as falling boulders and a voice as loud as thunder.

"FEE FI FO FUM, I SMELL THE BLOOD OF AN ENGLISHMAN!"

"I'll help you look for him," said the giant's wife. "If it's the boy who stole our little hen you shall have him for breakfast."

But Jack had hidden himself well, and in the end they had to give up looking.

After breakfast the giant called for his magic harp.

"Sing!" ordered the giant. And the harp sang sweetly.

Presently the giant's head began to nod. Soon he was asleep. Jack jumped from his hiding place, snatched up the magic harp, and started to run.

"Master! Master!" called the magic harp.

The giant woke with such a roar that the people in the land below the beanstalk thought the sky was falling in.

"FEE FI FO FUM. . ." he bellowed. "I *DO* SMELL THE BLOOD OF AN ENGLISHMAN. . ."

He ran after Jack with great lumbering, thundering steps. Jack was small and nimble, and had a good start. When he reached the top of the beanstalk he tucked the harp inside his shirt and began to climb down.

The beanstalk began to shake, and creak, and groan, as the angry giant followed him. . .

Faster went Jack . . . faster . . . and faster . . .

"Mother! . . ." he called as he neared the bottom. "Bring me an axe . . . quickly . . ."

He jumped to the ground and took the axe. He swung his arms as though he were the strongest man in the world, and with three hefty cuts the beanstalk came tumbling to the ground. There was a terrible roar as the giant fell. He made a hole so big, when he hit the ground, that both he and the beanstalk disappeared into it, and were lost forever.

As for Jack and his mother . . . well, they lived happily ever after with the hen who laid golden eggs, and the harp which sang beautiful songs. They were never poor again.

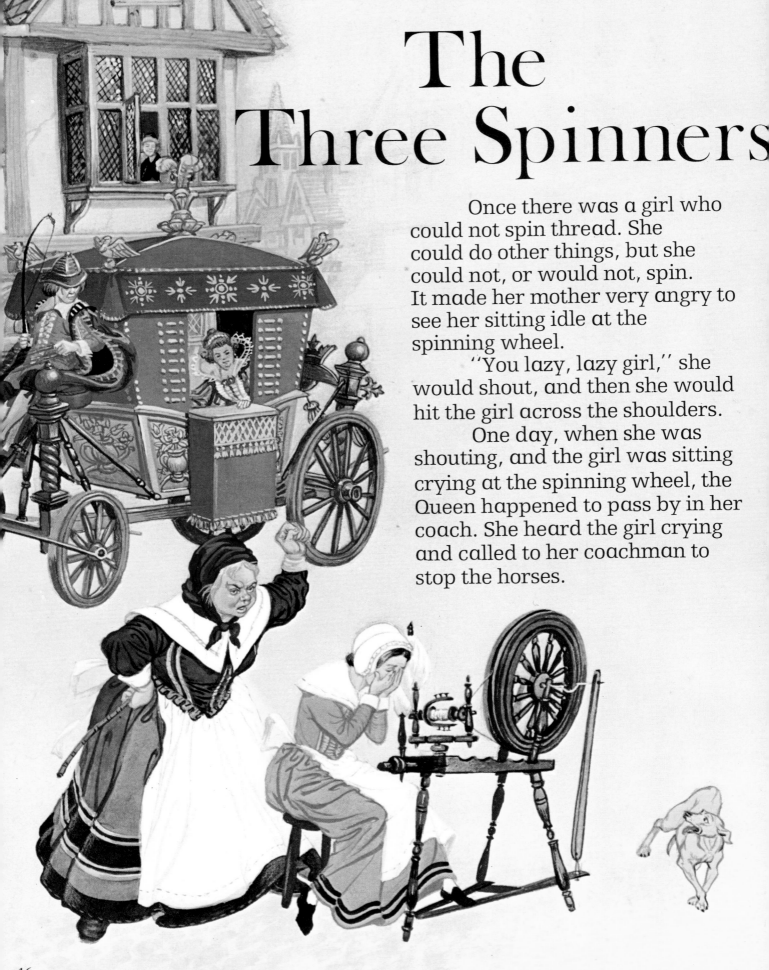

The Three Spinners

Once there was a girl who could not spin thread. She could do other things, but she could not, or would not, spin. It made her mother very angry to see her sitting idle at the spinning wheel.

"You lazy, lazy girl," she would shout, and then she would hit the girl across the shoulders.

One day, when she was shouting, and the girl was sitting crying at the spinning wheel, the Queen happened to pass by in her coach. She heard the girl crying and called to her coachman to stop the horses.

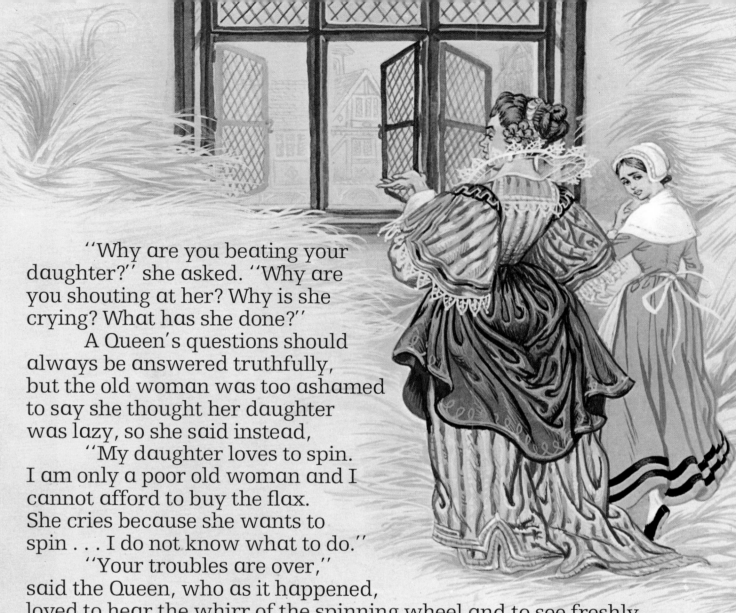

"Why are you beating your daughter?" she asked. "Why are you shouting at her? Why is she crying? What has she done?"

A Queen's questions should always be answered truthfully, but the old woman was too ashamed to say she thought her daughter was lazy, so she said instead,

"My daughter loves to spin. I am only a poor old woman and I cannot afford to buy the flax. She cries because she wants to spin . . . I do not know what to do."

"Your troubles are over," said the Queen, who as it happened, loved to hear the whirr of the spinning wheel and to see freshly spun thread. "I have plenty of flax at the palace. I will take your daughter home with me and she can spin as much as she likes."

The Queen took the girl to the palace and showed her three rooms which were full from floor to ceiling with unspun flax.

"Spin all THAT flax into thread, my dear, and you shall marry my son," said the Queen.

The poor girl did not know what to do. Of course she wanted to marry the prince, but how could she? She didn't know HOW to spin. For three whole days she sat and wept. On the third day the Queen came to see her.

"Why are you weeping child? Why haven't you started to spin?" asked the Queen.

The poor girl sobbed even harder.

"I brought you to the palace to spin flax," said the Queen sternly. "If there is no thread for me to see tomorrow you will be punished."

When the Queen had swept majestically from the room, the poor, sad girl stood at the window overlooking the street and cried as though her heart would break. Presently, through her tears, she saw three strange women walking along the pavement. One of them had a very broad, flat foot. One had a lip that hung down over her chin, and the third had an enormous thumb.

One of the women called up to the window and asked the girl why she was weeping.

"I do so want to marry the prince," she sobbed, "But first I must spin all this flax, and I do not know how to spin."

"If you will call us aunt and be unashamed of our strange appearance, and if you will invite us to sit with you at your wedding, we will help you," said the three women.

"I shall be glad to call you aunt," said the girl.

The three strange women were as good as their word. They slipped unnoticed into the palace and set to work. The one with the broad, flat foot worked the spinning wheel. The one with the lip which hung over her chin wetted the flax. And the one with the enormous thumb twisted the thread. Together they spun the finest thread the Queen had ever seen. She was impressed, though she thought the girl herself had done the spinning for the three strange women hid whenever they heard the Queen coming.

At last all the flax had been spun and it was time for the wedding. When the arrangements were being made, the girl said to the Queen,

''I have three aunts who have been very kind to me. May I invite them to the wedding and may they sit with me at the table?''

''Of course,'' said the Queen.

An invitation was sent, and on the day of the wedding the three strange women arrived and were welcomed kindly by the girl and the Prince.

"Tell me Aunt," said the Prince, who couldn't help noticing such things. "Why have you such a broad flat foot?"

"Because I tread a spinning wheel," said the first aunt.

"And how is it that you have such a long lip?" he asked the second aunt.

"Because I wet the spinning thread."

"And why have you such a large thumb?" asked the Prince of the third aunt.

"Because I twist the spinning thread," she answered.

The Prince looked at the three strange women, one with a broad flat foot, one with a lip that hung down over her chin and one with an enormous thumb, and then he looked at his beautiful bride.

"If that is what spinning thread does to a woman," he said, "I forbid you ever to touch a spinning wheel."

And so the girl married her prince, and the three spinners moved into the palace to take care of all the spinning. They loved spinning as much as the girl loved the prince and so everyone was happy.

The Brave Tin Soldier

Once, someone who was clever, made twenty-five tin soldiers from a single spoon. They were all painted in red and blue uniforms, and they all carried muskets over their shoulders. Except for the twenty-fifth, they were all exactly alike.

The twenty-fifth, and last, tin soldier was different simply because he was the last to be made. There hadn't been quite enough tin to finish him off and he had been left with one leg. Yet in spite of his handicap he was as brave, as smart, and as gallant as his companions, and fought many battles with them on the nursery floor.

Of all the other toys in the nursery, the little tin soldier most admired the dancer who stood in the doorway of the sparkling paste-board castle. She was as dainty and graceful as he was gallant and smart. She stood all the time on one leg, poised on the very tips of her toes, as dancers do. She held her other leg so high and straight behind her, that the little tin soldier, who had only seen her from the front, thought she had one leg like himself.

He often thought how wonderful it would be if she would consent to become his wife. But she was so graceful and aloof, and he was so shy in spite of being so gallant, that he did not dare to speak to her.

All he ever did was stand and stare.

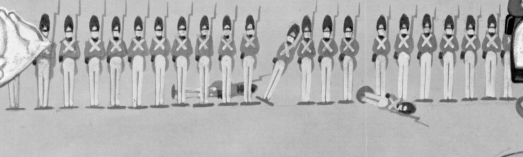

The toy conjurer was jealous when he saw the tin soldier staring at the little dancer.

"Stop staring" he said, "Or something will happen to you."

But nothing could deter the little tin soldier. He didn't take his eyes off the dancer for a moment. He didn't even turn his head to reply.

The morning after the conjurer had issued his warning the tin soldier was standing on the nursery windowsill. Now whether the wind was responsible, or whether the conjurer had something to do with it or not, no one knows, but suddenly the window blew open and before anyone could stop him the little tin soldier fell three storeys to the street below and landed on his head.

The boy who owned the twenty-five tin soldiers went to look for him, but he was wedged between two paving stones and could not be found, and when it began to rain the boy gave up the search.

He was rescued from his predicament by two urchins

who were sailing paper boats
in the torrent that raced
along the gutter.

    ''I've found a captain for
our ship,'' said one. He stood the
little tin soldier in the bows
of the boat and pushed it off.

    ''How stiffly he stands,''
said the other.

    The paper boat bobbed along
the gutter with the tin soldier
standing stiffly to attention.
He knew no other way of
standing. Suddenly the boat
was swept into the darkness of
a drain. It was so dark the tin
soldier could see nothing with
his eyes at all but in his
imagination he saw the little
dancer and hoped that she
hadn't forgotten him.
The boat sped faster and
faster. It rolled and it rocked
and still the little soldier stood
firmly to attention. He was a
credit to his regiment.
They would have been proud
had they seen him. And then,
just as the boat came to the
end of the drain and it grew light
the water fell, with a sudden gush,
into the canal.

The paper boat could hold out no longer. It began to fill with water. The little tin soldier sank lower and lower until only his head and the tip of his musket were above the water . . . and then they too disappeared.

He had almost reached the bottom of the canal, where he would have been lost for ever amongst the rubbish, when he was swallowed by a fish.

It had been dark inside the drain. It was twice as dark inside the fish. But even in the pitch black with no one to see him, the tin soldier still stood firmly to attention and kept his thoughts on the little dancer. He had almost given up hope of seeing her again when light suddenly burst in over his head like an exploding firework.

The fish had been caught and was being cleaned ready for cooking in the very house in which he had lived before his journey began. The maid recognised the little tin soldier and carried him to the nursery.

Everyone was anxious to see

the little soldier which had fallen from the window and ended up inside a fish but the little tin soldier himself only had eyes for the little dancer. She stood, aloof and graceful as ever, in front of the pasteboard castle.

And then, for no reason whatsoever, unless it was another trick of the jealous conjurer, one of the boys picked up the tin soldier and threw him into the fire. The tin soldier felt the heat of the flames engulf him and knew then that the little dancer would never become his wife.

But just at the moment when the little tin soldier finally gave up hope, a door opened, a draught caught the dancer and she flew straight into the fire beside him. She disappeared in a flurry of sparks . . . and the little tin soldier melted right away.

The next morning when the maid was clearing the ashes from the fireplace she found a charred tinsel rose and the tiny tin heart of the brave little tin soldier.

The Frog Prince

A beautiful Princess was playing with her golden ball one day when she dropped it. It rolled to the edge of a deep clear pool and fell, with hardly a splash, to the bottom. She could see it lying on the white stones but she could not reach it, and soon her tears began to fall.

"Why are you crying?" asked a voice close by. The only creature the Princess could see was a slender green frog. She was so astonished to hear a frog speak that she answered immediately.

"My golden ball is lying at the bottom of the pool." she said sadly.

"If I bring it back to you," said the frog, "Will you let me sit upon your chair, share your food when you eat, and lie upon your bed when I am tired?"

"Anything, anything at all." promised the Princess. "If only you will bring my ball to me."

But alas, when the frog had dived to the bottom of the deep clear pool and retrieved the golden ball, the ungrateful Princess snatched it from him and ran laughing across the palace lawns.

She did not give the frog, or the promise she had made, another thought.

Next morning however, when she was skipping along one of palace corridors, she met the slender green frog face to face, and she knew at once that he had come to claim his promise. She ran and hid behind her father, the King.

The King took her gently by the shoulders.

"You look very pale," he said, "Has something frightened you?"

The Princess told the King how the frog had returned her lost ball and of her promise to him and how, at that very moment he was hopping along the palace corridor.

"Please make him go away father," she pleaded.

But the King said sternly, "A promise is a promise and must be kept. Invite the frog to our table."

Because she was a dutiful daughter the Princess did as she was told and the King and his five daughters sat down to breakfast. The frog hopped to the side of the Princess who had played with the golden ball.

"May I sit upon your chair?" he asked.

The Princess lifted him onto the polished wooden arm.

"May I share your food?" asked the frog.

The Princess lifted him to the side of her plate.

When the frog had eaten he said,
"I am tired, may I lie upon your bed?"
The Princess carried the frog to her bedroom, but she was so afraid that the frog would hop onto the crisp white pillow upon which she lay her own head, that she put him on a chair in the corner of the room and hoped that that would do instead.

"I will tell your father you have not kept your promise," warned the frog.

The Princess burst into a flood of tears. She picked up the frog and threw him across the room to her bed.

"I have shared my chair with you . . . I have shared my food with you . . . must I really share my bed with you?" she sobbed.

And then, somehow, without her really seeing just how it happened, the slender green frog turned into a handsome young Prince who took her hand and gently wiped away her tears. He had been bewitched and because the Princess had shared her chair, her food and her bed with him, she had broken the spell.

The Princess who played with the golden ball, and the Prince who had been a frog, were married, of course, and they lived happily ever after in a land where promises were always kept.

Choosing a Wife

Once there was a shepherd who knew three sisters. They were all beautiful, and they were all kind, and he wanted to marry one of them. But which one? How could he choose one from the others when he liked them all equally?

"Invite them all to eat cheese with you," said the shepherd's mother, "and watch how they eat it."

The shepherd couldn't see how that could possibly help but he had to choose somehow or he would never be married, so he decided to do as his mother had suggested.

The three beautiful sisters came to the house and they, and the shepherd, sat together round the table, on which the shepherd's mother had placed a platter of cheese.

Each slice of cheese was smooth and creamy and shaped like a crescent moon. It looked very tempting, but at the widest edge of each slice was a layer of thick hard rind.

The shepherd watched carefully as the three sisters took cheese and began to eat.

The first sister couldn't wait to begin. She pushed the cheese into her mouth without bothering to take the rind off at all.

The second sister took a knife and cut the rind from the cheese it was true, but she cut away half the smooth creamy cheese with it.

The third sister took a knife and cut away the rind too, but she cut neither too little, nor too much. She didn't